Hey Jack!

Hey Jack! Books

The Crazy Cousins
The Scary Solo
The Winning Goal
The Robot Blues
The Worry Monsters
The New Friend
The Worst Sleepover
The Circus Lesson
The Bumpy Ride
The Top Team
The Playground Problem
The Best Party Ever
The Bravest Kid
The Big Adventure
The Toy Sale

First American Edition 2012
Kane Miller, A Division of EDC Publishing

Text copyright © 2012 Sally Rippin
Illustration copyright © 2012 Stephanie Spartels
Logo and design copyright © 2012 Hardie Grant Egmont
Design by Stephanie Spartels
Typesetting by Michaela Stone
First published in Australia in 2012 by Hardie Grant Egmont

For information contact:
Kane Miller, A Division of EDC Publishing
P.O. Box 470663
Tulsa, OK 74147-0663
www.kanemiller.com
www.edcpub.com
www.usbornebooksandmore.com

Library of Congress Control Number: 2012931653

Printed and bound in the United States of America
4 5 6 7 8 9 10
ISBN: 978-1-61067-122-4

Hey Jack!

The Scary Solo

By Sally Rippin

Illustrated by Stephanie Spartels

Kane Miller
A DIVISION OF EDC PUBLISHING

feels excited,
but a little bit sick

Legs feel
shaky

Jittery Mood

Chapter One

This is Jack.

This morning Jack is in a jittery mood. He wants to try for a solo in the school concert.

Jack likes singing,
but he feels too shy
to try out by himself.
So he has asked his
best friend Billie
to stand with him
while he sings.

Billie and Jack
practice singing in the
playground. They are
going to be **stars**!

3

"Next, please," calls Miss Winters. She is in charge of the school concert. Today she is choosing children for the solo parts.

Now it is Jack's turn to try out for a part.

Jack walks onto the stage.

4

Billie follows and
stands next to him.

Jack gets ready to sing.

But all of a sudden
Jack feels nervous
and wobbly. He
hops from one foot
to the other like
he has **ants in
his pants**.

The music starts. Jack
knows all the words,
but when he opens his
mouth, nothing comes out!

Jack stands with his mouth
wide-open. His tummy
squeezes tight.

Billie pokes him
in the ribs. "Hey, Jack!"
she says. "What's wrong?"

Jack closes his mouth.
It's no use. He is much
too **scared**
to sing on his own.
He feels silly
for even trying.

Miss Winters smiles kindly.
"Perhaps you can be
in the chorus, Jack.
Now, Billie, are you
trying out too?"

Billie nods. The music
starts, and Billie sings
loudly and clearly.

Jack feels cross and
sad at the same time.
He wishes he was
as brave as Billie.

"Well done, Billie!"
says Miss Winters when
Billie has finished.
"You can have a solo.
You sing very well."

Billie jumps up and
down in excitement.

Jack frowns. *But I can
sing too!* he thinks crossly.
*I can sing as well as Billie!
It's just that...*

Jack sighs. He hangs his head as he and Billie leave the hall.

Chapter Two

Billie runs out into the playground. Jack mooches along behind her.

"I can't believe it!" says Billie. "I got a solo!"

All the kids in the
playground stand
around Billie and
cheer for her.

Jack can see that Billie

is happy. He wants

to be happy too.

But right now he just

feels **cross**.

It was *his* idea to try out

for a solo in the school

concert. Not Billie's!

Jack scrunches up his

face and kicks the ground.

He feels a big, dark
monster inside him
grumbling to be let out.

"It's only a stupid
school concert!"
Jack shouts. "Who wants
to sing a solo anyway?
Only stupid people!"

Billie turns to Jack.
Her mouth drops open,
and her eyes grow wide.

"Jack!" she says. "That's
mean!"

Jack knows it's mean.
But he can't help it.
It's the big, grumpy
monster talking, not him.

18

Jack runs away from Billie to the other end of the playground.

For the rest of the day, Jack and Billie don't speak to each other. Jack glares at Billie, and she glares back.

Jack wants Billie to say sorry. He doesn't know why.

It's not fair that she got a solo in the school concert and he didn't.

But soon the **grumpy** monster in Jack's tummy goes away. He knows it is up to him to say sorry.

"I'm sorry for being mean," he says. "I'm happy that you got a solo, Billie. Really. Friends?"

"Friends," Billie says, smiling. "Forever."

"Hey, maybe you can
help me practice
my solo?" Billie adds.

Jack nods. "Sure," he says. "I'd like that."

All that week and the next, Jack helps Billie practice her solo for the musical.

They sing everywhere. In the kitchen and in the bathroom. In the backyard and in the house.

24

They sing as loud as rock stars – except when it's time for Billie's baby brother to have a nap. Then they sing baby Noah to sleep.

Jack can't wait for the concert!

Chapter Three

Finally the day of the school concert arrives. Jack and Billie's families drive to the school hall.

Billie and Jack are both wearing shiny silver tops. This is the costume their class is wearing for the concert.

Billie also has glitter
in her hair. She looks
just like a rock star.

Jack feels a teensy bit
jealous when
he sees Billie's hair.
He wishes he had
a solo too. He knows
being in the chorus
is an important job,
but it's not as exciting
as being a solo singer.

"Good luck, Billie!" their parents shout excitedly. "Hey, Jack! Good luck!"

Billie and Jack wave to their parents. They run backstage. Jack skips with excitement.

Soon it's time for
the concert to begin.

Every class is doing
a different song in
the concert. Jack and
Billie wait with their
class until it is their
turn to go on stage.

They wait and they wait.
Everyone is nervous
and **giggly**.

Sometimes Miss Winters pokes her head into the back room and frowns.

"Shhh!" she says with her finger on her lips. But this just makes everyone giggle even more.

Jack and Billie practice their song very quietly together.

Only two more songs, and they are on!

Jack feels his tummy flipping like a fish.

"OK!" Miss Winters whispers to Jack's class. "You're up next!"

Everyone in Jack's class runs onto the stage and stands in their positions. Billie stands in front, ready to sing her solo.

"Go, Billie!" Jack whispers.

The curtains open.

The music starts.

The spotlight shines

on Billie. Everyone

waits for her to sing.

Billie lifts up her

microphone. Her

mouth opens. But no

sound comes out!

Oh no! Jack thinks.

34

He knows *exactly*
what's wrong with Billie.
He knows that her legs
will be **wobbling**
like jelly.

The music stops.
Everybody looks at Billie,
waiting… waiting…

Poor Billie! thinks Jack.
She has no one to help her!

36

Billie is still standing
at the front, frozen.

Wait a second, thinks Jack.
I know this solo!

He runs to stand
next to Billie. Then he
grabs the microphone
and holds it between
himself and Billie.
He begins to sing.

The music starts
up again. Jack sings
loud and strong.
He knows all the words
by heart.

Billie stands with
her eyes wide-open.

Still singing, Jack
jabs her with
his elbow. He looks
at her and smiles.

Finally, she starts
to sing too. Quietly
at first, but then
louder and louder.

Soon Jack and
Billie are singing
at the top of
their voices.
Just like at home.

When Jack and
Billie's class has
finished the song,
everyone claps
and cheers.

People **Stomp**
their feet on the ground
and shout, "More! More!"

Jack and Billie's
parents cheer the
loudest of all.

Jack's smile stretches
across his face.
He looks at all those
cheering people.

41

He feels a big warm
burst of sunshine
in his chest.

He is a star!

43

Collect them all!